Frolic's Dance

by

Valerie Harms

Frolic the snowshoe hare opened her eyes to a sunny February morning. With a fluff of her white fur, she hopped eagerly out of the snow cave, where she'd rested all night. She scanned the gray sky and high treetops for owls or hawks. All she wanted was a chance to play undisturbed.

She bit off alder bark and mashed it with her teeth. Then she licked her fur and drew her ears down over her face to clean them with her paws. Satisfied, she stood up on her wide rear paws and leapt straight up in the air, wiggling her hips joyfully.

Just as she took a mouthful of snow to quench her thirst, she heard a branch snap. Her black-tipped ears flicked back and forth. Her sensitive nose picked up the smell of fox—a rare visitor in her part of Dry Bay, Alaska, and a deadly threat. Frolic held very still.

Sure enough, soon a young red fox appeared on the trail between the alder bushes. His delicate feet sank into the snow as he passed just opposite her. Suddenly he froze, waiting with one front paw held up. In a flash he pounced on a small vole, digging his sharp nose into the crusty snow to catch it. With his prey in his mouth, he turned to leave. For a moment, he seemed to look right at Frolic. Then he trotted away, waving his bushy tail gaily.

Shivering with relief, Frolic turned to look again for her favorite treat—willow twigs. As she hopped along the edge of some spruces, she spied the tracks of an ermine. Although the ermine is a very small weasel, its winter coat of white and its speed made it an enemy Frolic would just as soon avoid. She dodged an old tree stump, where the ermine was likely to live. But no ermine appeared to disturb the silence.

She bravely bounded out into an open field, where the sun's rays were unshaded by trees. The warm sun beating on her back made her feel frisky. She leaped into the air, twisting her furry hips in a little wiggle.

But just as she started to dance, a wiry, stub-tailed lynx came streaking toward her. Nothing frightened her more than his fierce face with its fringe of fur ruff. He was her worst enemy, for his main source of food was the snowshoe hare.

Frolic had to think quickly of a way to outwit the lynx. First, she ran in a big circle, then a smaller one, throwing snow up behind her. But the lynx was nearly as fast as she was. He too had large feet like snowshoes. He was so close she could feel his breath hot on her haunches. Her only hope was to tire him or lose him.

Frolic tried another trick. She hurled herself into the air and made a sharp right turn. Before the lynx could stop, she had darted under some bushes. Here she froze, panting for breath. The lynx knew she hadn't gotten far. He sank down on his belly to wait, growling and showing his claws. Frolic worried. If she let the lynx rest too long, he would be fresh again and harder to escape.

The lynx suddenly bounded forward to startle the hare from her hiding place. The trick worked. Frolic plunged through thick brambles, leaving behind her the network of familiar trails that she and other hares had made before winter even started.

On they ran, through tall marsh grass growing on the banks of a river. The snow was moist from the sun, making for easy traction, so the lynx stayed right on her heels. Lost and tired, Frolic ran for a long time without looking back. Just as she was about to drop, she realized she could no longer hear the lynx's heavy breathing. Somewhere behind her he had given up the chase.

She continued over the crest of a hill looking for a place where she could safely stop and rest. With sides heaving, she stood on a knoll. Lifting her head, she found to her surprise that she was very near the ocean. Here the river she'd been following was nearly covered with thick ice, reaching far out into the sea. She hopped toward some rocks and bushes. A mountain goat was picking his way along the rocks that were coated with salt from the sea spray. He was licking salt from the rocks. He was large—nearly three feet high—with a shaggy coat and sharp, black horns curving backward. He had a wise face and a fine long beard under his chin.

Since he looked friendly, Frolic hopped over. "Can you tell me where I am?" she asked.

The mountain goat looked calmly at Frolic. "You are near the Alsek River where it joins the Pacific Ocean," he replied. "I just followed it myself from the mountains. There is so much snow up there it is hard to find something to eat."

"I usually avoid the water," Frolic said. "It is too open and too easy to spot a hare. But I ran here to get away from a lynx."

"A race well run," congratulated the goat.

At the sound of splashing Frolic spun around. A sea otter stood near them in the shallows of the ocean water. He had a sleek, narrow body and whiskers. He lay back and swam with his hands folded over his belly. Then he did a backflip dive. Coming up, he said, "I bet you can't do that."

Frolic laughed, liking him at once. "I bet you are right," she replied. "I swim only if I have to. Would you join me on land instead?"

"No thank you," he sang. "But what is your name? And what is your game?"

"Frolic," she answered, wriggling her hips. "What's yours? And do you always rhyme?"

"Some of the time," the otter said. "My name is Scamp because I love to play."

Just then a moose calf trotted over on long knobby legs to join them. Her face was very long and her nose velvety brown. She had wide ears flopping out to the sides of her face. "I'm Beezle," she said in a warm, husky voice.

"Hello," the mountain goat said. "I am Sage. It seems this sunny day has brought a number of us to the ocean."

Beezle stamped a hoof and snorted. "I have just run away from my mother. She always has so many lessons for me to learn. There is never enough time for me to play. I just left her back in the marsh."

Frolic said, "At least you have someone who wants to protect you. My mother has so many new litters of baby hares each year. She sends us out on our own when we are very young."

Beezle's ears flapped impatiently. "But you have independence," she said. "I am under my mother's nose all day."

The older Scamp said, "Soon enough you'll be on your own, all alone. Later this spring your mother will have a new baby moose to care for."

Frolic fretted. "It seems just yesterday I was a baby. A hare's life is so short. So many of us get caught and eaten up. It seems so much of my life is spent escaping death."

Sage stopped chewing his cud and said, "It's a law of nature that some must die so others can live. This may seem harsh, Frolic, but some say that no one really dies. We simply change form."

Frolic, Beezle and Scamp listened alertly.

"Change form into what?" asked Frolic.

"It is said that snowshoe hares change into snowflakes after they die and drift over the hills. That is why each snowflake is different."

"How lovely," sighed Frolic. Scamp clapped his hands. But Beezle shook her head, puzzled.

"I'd be an awfully big snowflake," she said. Distracted, she raised her long nose into the breeze. Her short mane bristled. "I smell bear upstream." All of the animals looked where Beezle's nose was pointing.

"I smell bear too, Beezle," said Sage. "So I think I'll head back to the mountain. I hope to see you again." He trotted away with short, sure steps, his shaggy haunches swaying. Frolic froze, hoping her white fur blended into the background of snow. Beezle edged further and further out on the covered ice-banks of the river, right where it met the ocean.

Upstream, a bulky, blue-gray bear emerged from its den to see if spring had come. The bear looked up and down the river. After a few irritated shakes of its head, the bear lumbered back into its cave.

"Whew," said Frolic. "He must not be ready to wake up yet."

Scamp was swimming along the ocean bank, as close as possible to Beezle. "Watch out, Beezle," he shouted. "Out here the ice can break away from the banks."

Beezle picked her way along the jagged ice. Her nose was carried high, as if to say that she could think for herself, thank you.

"The bear is gone, Beezle," called Scamp. "Get off the ice <u>now</u>. Soon it will be too late."

Suddenly, Beezle's legs went flying up from the ice, and she landed with a great thud. A loud crackling sound began. The chunk of ice Beezle was lying on began to drift away from the bank. Beezle seemed too dazed to move.

Beezle tried to stand up, but the ice was smooth as glass. She could not get a foothold. She fell again and again.

Scamp swam frantically toward Frolic. Frolic hopped to meet him. Scamp squealed, "You've got to get help. Only you can do it. If the ice that Beezle is riding on goes into the ocean, we'll never see Beezle again."

Frolic's heart pounded. It would be very risky to make any noises that would attract a lynx or fox. But every second the river current was carrying Beezle further and further away. She began to drum with her large hind feet. First, she faced north, then south, then east, then west, drumming and drumming a message that would vibrate along the frozen ground.

Suddenly, with a clattering of hooves, a huge moose appeared. In a glance she could see what had happened. She trotted over the rough peaks of ice toward Beezle. "Beezle," she called. "Come back!" She ran along the bank, trying to keep up with the drifting ice floe and shouting, "Beezle, jump!"

In the water Scamp circled Beezle's ice raft. Beezle raised her head at the sight of her mother and gave a long moan. She seemed to be frozen with fear.

Beezle's mother leaped into the icy water. She stroked swiftly toward the ice floe. Getting behind it, she shoved against it with her strong chest. At first she made no headway against the current of the river. The ice raft was being swept toward the ocean. But Mother Moose heaved and slowly changed the direction of the ice raft. She steered it near shore. "Jump, Beezle, jump and swim for shore," she commanded.

Beezle looked as if she could not believe her mother's words.

Suddenly, Beezle's mother bellowed—very, very loudly.

As if gathering strength from her mother's tone, Beezle at last pushed off from the ice. Her hind legs kicked the ice backward, so she did not quite make the shore. She thrashed about in the shallow water. Her mother nudged her onto the shore while Scamp chattered and clapped.

The mother moose nuzzled her calf lovingly. Frolic danced in circles around them.

"Who was drumming?" asked Beezle's mother. "I had been looking for Beezle, and when I heard those warning sounds I knew where to go."

"That was Frolic," said Scamp. "She saved the day. Hooray! Hooray!"

"She certainly did," said Beezle's mother. "Thank you, Frolic. What a brave, good friend you are!" Frolic beamed, proud to be a heroine.

Scamp drew near to Frolic and said, "Your life may be short and dangerous, but it is more valuable than you think."

"That's right," said Beezle. "You saved my life."

"I think we will just go home now for some rest," Mother Moose said. Beezle waved her ears in goodbye.

Frolic and Scamp watched as Mother Moose and Beezle disappeared over a frosted hill. Scamp said, "Now if you don't mind, it's time for my nap." He lay back with a streamer of kelp wrapped around him as an anchor. It looked just like a blanket.

Frolic watched in silence as her friend fell asleep. With a shake of her tail, she darted away over the snow as fast as she could to find her way home before dark.

That night there was a full moon. Frolic and her brothers and sisters and friends gathered together. Safe and unbothered at last, they played leapfrog and tag for hours.

Happy and tired, she looked up at the stars. The moon glistened on the crusty snow. The air smelled crisp and clean. Slowly Frolic began to dance. First, she put her fears into her steps, then her tears. Next, she danced for her new friends. Finally, she spun around to celebrate the surprises life gave her.

To all animals, everywhere.

The author gratefully acknowledges the technical assistance of Lowell Suring, of the Department of Wildlife and Fisheries in Alaska, and Dr. Charles Handley of The Smithsonian Institution.

Points of Interest in This Book

pp. 2, 3. Sitka alders, paperbirch, red fox, meadow vole
p. 6.   lynx, highbush-cranberry
p. 8.   mountain goat
p. 10. sea otter
p. 12. moose calf
p. 14. (an Eskimo legend about snowshoe hares)
p. 15. a black bear (called 'glacier bear' in its blue phase)
p. 29. kelp

———————————

Text copyright © 1989 by Soundprints Corporation and The Smithsonian Institution. Illustrations copyright © 1989 by Soundprints Corporation, a subsidiary of Trudy Corporation, 165 Water Street, Norwalk, CT 06856. Manufactured by Horowitz/Rae Book Manufacturers, Inc. Designed by Judy Oliver, Oliver and Lake Design Associates. First edition 10 9 8 7 6 5 4 3 2 1.

Library of Congress Cataloging-in-Publications Data
Harms, Valerie   Frolic's Dance
Summary: A snowshoe hare, hunted by lynx and other predators, discovers courage and friendship in an attempt to help a young moose calf in trouble.
1.   Hares—juvenile literature   [1. Hares]
1.   Harms, Valerie.   11. Title.
ISBN: 0-924483-01-6